A DANGEROUS JOURNEY TO STARDOM

NII KOJO ADDY

A DANGEROUS JOURNEY TO STARDOM

Publisher
Vike Springs Publishing Ltd.
www.vikesprings.com

First Edition
ISBN-13: 978-1-8380718-5-1- E-book
ISBN-13: 978-1-8380718-7-5- Paperback

Printed in the
United Kingdom and United States of America

For Bookings and Speaking Engagements, Contact Us:
Nii - Email: nii_addy2000@yahoo.com or admin@vikesprings.com
Nii's books are available at special discounts when purchased in bulk for promotions or as donations for educational and training purposes.

Limit of Liability/ Disclaimer of Warranty

DEDICATION

This book is dedicated to my family and everyone who has gone through the indignity of crossing the Mediterranean for a better life.

ACKNOWLEDGEMENTS

I would like to take the opportunity to acknowledge the following people for their help and support in my life: Philip Anderson (for his help in the research), Nii Obuama Addy, Tina Abujajah, Mr Ebenezer Addy, Mrs Phyllis Addy, Nii Kpani Addy, Naa akuyea Shika pappoe, Rosemary Allotey Annan, Sheila Agbotse, Pastor Samuel Bentil and Shana Kaye Bernard.

Thank you to Victor Kwegyir and the team at Vike Springs Publishing Ltd., London UK for the professional comprehensive services: editing, proofreading, formatting/layout, cover design, worldwide publishing and distribution, printing, and marketing of this book.

Table of Contents

Introduction

This book tells the story of how countless Africans perish while crossing the Mediterranean. It's about a young footballer and his best friend who pay a fortune to agents who smuggles people across the desert.

Chapter One

Paa Nii Roland hurried into his room to pick up his shoe box. It was where he hid his football prize money, along with the earnings he got from the matches he played in from time to time.

The earnings were a pittance. Sometimes, if his side for the day lost, he wouldn't even get paid at all. The 'winner takes all' rule applied.

But despite the miserable earnings, Paa Nii had managed to save thousands in the shoe box. And he had hidden the true amount of his savings from his mum.

Paa Nii's dribbling and scoring ability was years ahead of his peers. His mother, who was semi-illiterate, hardly ever followed the news. As such, she had no idea her son had won the grand prize of five thousand dollars during the recent, lavishly-sponsored interschool regional football championship.

Paa Nii dreamt of leaving Ghana and crossing the Mediterranean, where he would have a real chance of making it as a football star. His best friend, Muftao Aziz, a.k.a Shaka, had suggested that they make their way to Europe, in an attempt to follow their dreams. Though Paa Nii knew it a dangerous – and perhaps foolish

– suggestion, he also knew that if he was to make it as a footballer, he had no choice but to try.

With two thousand dollars tucked in his pocket, he headed off to Shaka's place. They intended to take a part payment to the so called 'connection man' who would set up their trip to Italy via the Sahara Desert.

'Why are you late? I've been waiting for ages,' Shaka scolded Paa Nii when he arrived at the meeting point.

Paa Nii shuffled uncomfortably. The bar was isolated and there were a couple of shady looking guys around. He nervously tucked his tightly-folded money into the inner pocket of his tracksuit.

Shaka ordered two bottles of Coke while they waited for the connection man to show up. Paa Nii had no idea what the person they were waiting for looked like, but when a tall man strode out of the staffroom behind the bar, Shaka leapt suddenly to his feet. The connection man spoke in a husky voice, introducing himself as Mr. Doudu.

'Nice to meet you,' Paa Nii replied sheepishly. His confidence in the whole scheme completely drained as he sized the man up.

Doudu's green checked shirt was un-ironed and his hair looked unkempt. He smelt as though he hadn't showered for days!

Paa Nii struggled to hide his grimace as he noticed Mr. Doudu's front pockets were torn. The guy looked like a tramp. How could he possibly be the man to get them to Europe? He looked like he needed a trip to greener pastures more than they did.

Shaka noticed the change in Paa Nii's demeanour on their way home.

'What's on your mind?' he asked.

Paa Nii sighed. 'I don't feel comfortable giving this emaciated-looking guy my money.'

Shaka waved his concerns away. 'I know loads of people he has helped. And besides, do you really think you're that good a judge of character? Remember when you went behind my back to deal with that fake visa contractor?'

Paa Nii shook his head in disgust when he remembered how he had been swindled two thousand dollars by the fake contractor.

He had been devastated after the first visa attempt, and he'd thought of giving up, but he knew the only way of following his dreams was to attempt to cross the Mediterranean to Italy. There, he would definitely find his way to a big football club. He felt sure of it.

Paa Nii's childhood had not been easy. His father, Peter Akwetey Roland, was an accountant who had left his mother soon after he was born. Even though he visited them intermittently, he hardly gave them any support. But Paa Nii's mother had instilled her strong Christian values of forgiveness in her son, so he didn't harbour any hard feelings against his father.

His mother, unable to support her child with her Kenkey business, had packed up and moved to Suyani in the Brong Ahafo region, to engage in sustenance farming.

Paa Nii's mind was still racing when he got home. The house was a two-bedroom mud hut his mother rented from one of the farmers she worked for. Paa Nii lay on his sleeping mat and stared up at the ceiling of his tiny bedroom.

He wondered whether he was doing the right thing. He had already lost so much money at the hands of the fake visa contractor. And now he was going to give another chunk of his savings to Mr. Doudu? He seemed he should know better, like the 'once bitten twice shy' cliche suggested.

Paa Nii had been a child prodigy, but he'd not had the chance to join any youth teams till his early teens.

His mother had forced him to work hard at school, and to help on the farm after his classes. She believed it would teach him essential life skills.

She felt football was an unwelcome distraction. She didn't have a clue that her son's alias, 'World Pele' meant he was a very talented footballer. Things got really bad financially, so Paa Nii had to play truant and play pick-up games for money. Sometimes he had to run away to Techiman, the biggest town in the region, to prevent being spotted by his mother's friends.

He caught the eye of a lot of youth football agents; his only dilemma was how to break the news to his mother.

This went on for a while, till he met a supporter who assured him he could get Paa Nii a scholarship to St. Augustine's College in Cape Coast.

His mother burst into tears of joy when Paa Nii told her of the scholarship. Her underlying anger at Paa Nii's truancy instantly vaporised from her mind.

She hadn't been happy when she had discovered her son had been playing football all this time. She'd been under the impression he was helping Shaka sell shoes at the market after school.

Even though the money he brought home to support her was vital, her main concern was his academic progress. She felt that was their way out of poverty. But after hearing the good news of his admission to one of the best secondary schools in the country, she decided football wasn't so bad after all.

But when he finished school, Paa Nii got a cruel shock. He was dropped from the national Under-17s team. He knew he was by far the best player on the squad. He'd gotten a call-up because of his extraordinary skills and good scoring ability at school.

He couldn't make sense of being left out of the final squad.

'I told you, if you're not rich, you can't buy a place on the squad,' Shaka alleged.

Paa Nii shook his head. 'That can't be right. I got five school mates in the squad and none of them are rich.'

'Well, we have to take action,' Shaka suggested.

'What do you have in mind?' Paa Nii queried.

'There's this national juvenile tournament that's being sponsored by all the big companies,' Shaka told him. 'The best player and the top goal scorer will get an unprecedented two thousand five hundred dollars each.' He grinned at Paa Nii. 'You'll win both.'

Paa Nii forced a laugh. 'You must be joking.'

Shaka shook his head, his eyes growing serious. 'Not only are you going to win, but I'll place bets with loads of people to raise money for both of us.'

'What will we use the money for?' Paa Nii queried.

'For a visa connection to Europe,' Shaka blurted out.

'Europe?' Paa Nii repeated. 'What are you talking about?'

Shaka shook his head, clearly irritated by Paa Nii's naivety. 'You want a career as a footballer, that's where you need to be.' He gave a short laugh. 'What, you didn't think you could actually stay here in Ghana did you?'

Paa Nii realised Shaka was right. He did want a career as a professional footballer. And it was not something he could do in Ghana. And so he'd set about trying to make his journey to Europe a reality.

Paa Nii had cast a forlorn figure when it had turned out the visa connection was a complete fraud. The worst part was, he had not told Shaka about it.

One of his old teammates had recommended Dr. Dre. He was supposed to be a magician when it came to hooking people up with visas for any country on earth. When Paa Nii met him at the plush Labadi Beach hotel, Dr. Dre promised to set him up in Spain. He boasted he could even get him a trial at Barcelona. His suave looks and neatly trimmed beard made him stand out as a successful visa contractor.

After collecting a part payment of one thousand eight hundred dollars, he gave Paa Nii fake documents to take to the Dutch embassy. Dr. Dre stressed that if Paa Nii got to Holland, he could easily get him a trial at Ajax and later Barcelona. 'The two clubs are traditionally linked. From Cruyff to Van Gaal. They have the same playing philosophy,' Dre stressed.

On the day of the supposed interview at the Dutch Embassy, Paa Nii eagerly gulped down his breakfast and quickly boarded a taxi. He had travelled from Suyani overnight and had not slept at all.

There was a long queue at the embassy when he arrived. He paid the driver and walked to the kiosk where Dre had asked him to wait. It suddenly dawned on him he had not received his passport yet. Dre had probably already presented it for him, he thought.

Paa Nii wiped the beads of sweat from his forehead. It was almost eleven and Dre had not shown up yet. The contractor had promised to meet him at ten, so he could coach him on what to say when the interview started.

'It's just a formality, I have all the counsellors in my pocket.' Paa Nii remembered Dre's words. He wiped the sweat off his forehead again. It came more from anxiety than the scorching heat.

He approached the security guard at the side gate. He recalled Dre saying his inside contact was called Sulley. He'd probably get some answers if he had a word with him. He realised his hands were shaking as he approached the gate.

'I need to speak to Mr Sulley,' he told the guard in a trembling voice.

The guard eyed him curiously. 'Who are you?'

'Dr. Dre sent me,' Paa Nii managed. 'I've got an interview. Can I speak with Mr. Sulley?'

'Dr. Dre?' the guard repeated. 'I got no idea what you're talking about. And there's no one called Sulley here.'

Paa Nii had burst into tears when he got back from his ill-fated trip to the Dutch Embassy. He was glad his mother was not back from the farm yet. He had paid out one thousand eight hundred dollars to Dre, who had vanished into thin air. His phone was off and the directions to his house had turned out to be false.

He had told his mum he was travelling to Cape Coast to check on his old school coach. She had no idea of his scheme with Dre or the fact that he had had such a huge sum of money on him. The worst part was when he'd been chased off the embassy grounds like a criminal. He had gone ballistic when he'd realised Dre was not going to show up and there was no interview – and certainly no Sulley on the staff list.

Now, as he lay on his sleeping mat, thinking about Mr. Doudu, Paa Nii couldn't help but wonder if he was making the same mistake. He nearly jumped out of his skin when he heard his mother shouting his name.

'I've been calling you for a long time,' she scolded.

'I'm sorry, I dozed off,' Paa Nii lied. 'I was feeling a bit tired.'

'Okay, come and help me prepare supper, and we will have a talk about university prospects or future options.'

Paa Nii was dreading that part. He doubted he would pass his Senior High School exam. Even if he did, he wanted to play football. It was imperative he travelled abroad. He knew his mother would object to him playing professional football right after secondary school. '*What if you get injured?*' He could almost hear her voice in his head.

They sat down to dinner, Paa Nii chewing his food whilst in deep thought. His mind was miles away and he nodded sheepishly at whatever his mother said, without hearing her words. He fixed his eyes on her while she went on and on. It was almost like he could see her lips moving without hearing a word. He knew this would be the last time he laid eyes on her for many, many days. Shaka had promised the crossing of the Mediterranean wasn't as dangerous as it sounded. But then again, when had Shaka ever been right about anything?

'Paa Nii, I've asked you three times whether you want some more. Where has your mind been?'

He shook his head. 'I'm full.'

His mother's jaw dropped in surprise. He had never turned down an extra helping in his life.

His mother bawled her eyes out when he told her the truth later that night. He could not bear the idea of leaving without telling her where he was going. Besides, he would turn eighteen in two months. He was old enough to make his own decisions.

'I'm a man now, I don't have to lie about this any longer,' he insisted.

'I'll let you turn professional if that's what it takes to get you scouted,' his mother said, wiping her eyes. 'Just stay here. Please.'

Paa Nii looked down, unable to meet her eyes. 'It's too late for that now, Ma. Besides, I don't want to play here, all that juju and weird rituals. I just want to head to Europe.' He held his mum's hands to prevent her from collapsing. 'Everything will be fine. God-willing I'll find a club and send you some money. Everything is going to be great.'

Chapter Two

The next morning, Paa Nii tiptoed out of the house before dawn. He had had a last glimpse of his mother while she slept. Though it broke his heart to leave without saying goodbye, he couldn't bear to see her cry again. He was at the point of no return.

Paa Nii was dead silent when they boarded the mini Toyota Hiace bus. Shaka had given up on trying to get a word out of him. Doudu had made arrangements for their journey to be as smooth as possible. The first part of the journey was to take a bus to Ouagadougu in Burkina Faso.

Doudu had taught the boys how to hide their money in their underwear till they got to Libya. Their night was going to be a hectic one: from Ouagadougou they had to take another bus to Niger where the dangerous part of the journey would start – the actual crossing of the Sahara Desert to Libya.

Paa Nii had used some of their money to buy food and other essentials, and had heeded Doudu's advice for them to be economical.

Paa Nii had been surprised to find Doudu actually seemed to care. Apparently, it was his passion to see people from poor backgrounds make it to Europe. He'd even given them a major discount of one thousand five hundred dollars each.

Shaka glanced at his friend, wondering what was on his mind. The journey would take about ten hours – he hoped he could get a word out of him by then. The bus had about sixteen passengers, and most of them were dozing off, so he decided to get some shut-eye for the journey ahead.

*

Paa Nii came back to life after the first rest stop. Shaka was delighted he was back to himself. 'You can see everyone looks confident, Nii Nii.'

Paa Nii managed a smile. 'Well I guess there is nothing to fear after all. I just miss my mum already.'

On the bus, they befriended a guy who looked like he was in his late twenties. Alex claimed he had made the trip before. Apparently, he had been deported after he was caught working in a clothes factory after five years in Italy.

'It's a bit tough during the desert crossing, but once it's done the agents will get good boats for us,' he told them. 'I hope you have enough money on you.'

'Yes,' Shaka blurted out. He winced when he felt Paa Nii's sharp nudge to his ribs.

Paa Nii observed Alex was being inquisitive, and his instincts told him to be discreet. He glanced around, taking mental notes about the passengers. He noticed five ladies who kept to themselves. They were smallish, so he found it difficult to determine whether they were teenagers or in their twenties.

The other male passengers looked eager to make the trip. He guessed they had gone through hell to raise enough money. His attention returned to Alex. He talked a bit too much and was certainly one to keep an eye on.

*

Paa Nii sighed with relief when they got to Ouagadougu. His long legs were cramped, thanks to the lack of space between the seats. At six-foot-one, he was a bit taller than most people.

He hoped it wouldn't make him too conspicuous among the other passengers. He had been a bit nervous when they had been stopped earlier at the Burkinabe border.

The border patrol agents had looked unfriendly and they'd had AK 47s strapped on their shoulders. A few glanced at him, making him nervous, but Paa Nii's anxiety had turned out to be unfounded. A few whispers between the driver and the agents and they were off again.

The group waited in Ouagadougu until nightfall for their new agent. At each stage, Doudu had said, there would be a new agent who would ensure the next step of their journey went ahead without any problems.

The new agent introduced himself as Suleiman. He was lanky and wore dark glasses, even though it was past sunset. He had a French accent, but his broken English was good enough for Paa Nii to understand. He explained that they had to change to a bigger bus as two more groups would be joining them.

After several hours, a 1990 lime green Tata LP1512 finally arrived to pick up the now merged groups. Paa Nii had counted fifty eight after the other two groups had joined them; they were Burkinabes.

Their next destination was the Niger border. There they could restock their food and water supplies. Suleiman told them their point of entry into the Sahara would be Agadez. The crossing would be through secret routes to avoid rogue rebels and the military. Paa Nii's high spirits dipped again when it dawned on him that this could be dangerous. He was not sure what they had gotten themselves into.

Despite his unease, Paa Nii slept throughout the journey. They were due to arrive at the Niger border at dawn. He opened his eyes to loud angry voices outside. Sunlight was flooding the windows of the bus. He shook Shaka's shoulder to wake him.

'What's happening?' Paa Nii asked edgily. He tried to peer out the window of the bus.

'It's the border forces,' Shaka told him matter-of-factly, rubbing the sleep from his eyes.

'Are you sure?'

'Yes of course.' Shaka pointed out the window. 'Can't you read the sign?'

Paa Nii's eyes widened in fear. 'What are we going to do?'

'Everyone calm down,' Suleiman said as he strode through the bus towards the door. 'I'll go talk to them. You won't have to show any ID.'

Paa Nii sat with his forehead pressed to the window, his heart thundering. He watched as the border patrol officers led Suleiman to their shed. He came out after a few minutes, smiling and chatting with them. It was obvious he had bribed them. Paa Nii let himself breathe.

Suleiman climbed back on the bus, giving them a wide grin. 'Everything is okay. From here to Agadez we will have no more problems.'

Chapter Three

The boys were oblivious to the fact that things were about to change. They were young, exuberant and naïve to how dangerous this journey actually was. Shaka had heard how great Europe was and how he could become rich and build a mansion back home if he worked hard.

He was an orphan who had been raised by his aunt. He had learned to fend for himself at a tender age, hence he had a number of street friends who had introduced him to a lot of bad stuff. But his life had taken a turn for the better when Paa Nii and his mother had moved to Suyani from Accra. Shaka had left most of his friends and had started illegal sports betting, knowing Paa Nii's side would always win – unless of course, the match was fixed.

His lust for Europe was fuelled by Sosu, a shoe shine boy who had crossed the Mediterranean to Italy. Sosu had come back to Ghana successful; he'd bought a beautiful five-bedroom house and a car for his mother.

Since his early teens, Shaka had been determined to make a trip to Europe, by land, sea or air – whatever it took. Paa Nii's influence also made him attend technical school after his junior secondary education. He wasn't brilliant enough to go to the so-called top schools.

He hustled at the market during holidays, peddling all sorts of stuff to help finance his dream. And after years of struggling and dreaming, they were finally on their way. Europe was in sight.

But when the bus began to move again in the direction of Agadez, Shaka felt something in his gut. Something was just not right. He hardly ever complained like Paa Nii did, but when his instincts kicked in, he always trusted them.

*

The boys tucked into the last of the food in their backpacks. They were famished, as they had barely eaten for two days. 'I've never been this hungry in my life, and I'm a hustler,' Shaka said jokingly.

'You're just crazy.'

'It's the truth.'

'Well, we need to go on that fast now that we are in Niger,' Paa Nii reminded him.

Doudu had told the boys to go on a fast to help their bodies adjust to the rigours of travelling through the desert.

'Wow, I'd completely forgotten about that,' Shaka said despondently.

'It will be over in three days,' Paa Nii encouraged him. He lowered his voice. 'Let's hide our money when we get to Agadez, just like Doudu told us to do.'

Shaka nodded in agreement.

*

The boys waited a couple of hours at the Nigerian border town of Maradi. A couple of other groups joined them. Paa Nii heard French, Arabic and other languages around him. There were now over one hundred and twenty people in their group. Suleiman explained they were waiting for trucks to come and take them to Agadez. Agadez was the last ghetto on the trail before crossing the desert.

'If you have enough money, pay me and I'll find you a nice place to stay,' Suleiman told them.

'That's not fair,' a young lady protested. 'I thought the money we'd already paid covered everything.'

'Will do or die my friend,' Suleiman snapped.

Paa Nii glanced at Shaka. His friend was pacing back and forth through the dust, arms folded across his chest.

'What's wrong?' he asked. 'Are you worried about money? Cos we've got plenty.'

Shaka forced a smile. 'Yeah. It'll be fine.'

But Paa Nii could tell something was bothering him. He waited for Shaka to say more, but he was silent. Paa Nii patted him on the back to assure him everything would be all right.

*

Paa Nii slept throughout the journey to Agadez. The road trip had finally taken its toll. After hours rattling around in the back of the truck, they finally got to Agadez, the so-called gateway to the Sahara. It was an ancient town which had been a resting point for traders for centuries. When they got to the ghetto, everyone climbed down from the trucks.

There were many ghettos of this kind strewn along the trail to Libya. Migrants were housed in the ghettos, crammed together between roofs that looked as though they would crumble with the faintest breath of wind. Paa Nii was taken aback by the number of people in the ghetto.

'Some of these people have been waiting for months to cross,' Alex explained when he noticed the astonishment on Paa Nii's face.

'How long can one wait for?' he asked, wary of the answer.

'From months to years – or you can be enslaved if you can't pay for the rest of the trip.'

Shaka's eyes widened. 'How many times do we have to pay during the journey? The other group members told me they have had multiple roll calls and paid more money after each one.'

Alex nodded. 'Many more will follow as we near Libya.'

The ghetto was strewn with militia and rough looking thugs. Suleiman approached and introduced them to a '*passeur*' named Monsieur Loe. *Passeurs* were expert smugglers who knew the desert like the backs of their hands. They knew the backroads and places to avoid being tracked by rebels or government anti-trafficking forces.

A long list was handed to him, and the whole group stood in terrified silence. Tall and brutish, Loe's large glasses made him look like a mean death row warden calling out the names of people about to be hanged.

Slowly, Loe read name after name from the list. Paa Nii stared in horror as the people whose names were read out were pulled away by muscular thugs. Some wailed in fear, while others struggled against them, to no avail. Trembling, Paa Nii turned to look at Shaka. He could tell his friend was shaken. Shaka, Paa Nii knew, had realized the coin had turned and their journey was about to take a turn for the worse.

And then, in his gravelly voice, Loe read out both Paa Nii and Shaka's names. Paa Nii stepped forward on shaky legs. His heart thundered as the thugs came towards them.

This was what he had wanted, Paa Nii told himself. He wanted his name to be called out, so that he might cross the Sahara and make his way to Europe. But as the thugs grabbed his arms in a vice-like grip, his thoughts tangled in terror.

He and Shaka were dragged away from the rest of the group and shoved in the direction of the ghetto. Two of the burly men glared down at Paa Nii with murderous eyes. Out of the corner of his eye, he could see Shaka reaching beneath his waistband for the bag of money he had hidden in his underwear.

Paa Nii suddenly remembered Shaka's words: '*The other group members told me they have had multiple roll calls and paid more money after each one.*' These thugs wanted more money. Perhaps if he gave it to them, they would let him live.

Hands shaking, Paa Nii dug a hand beneath his waistband, searching for his carefully hidden money. He felt as though his legs would give way at any moment. Finally, he produced a wad of money and shoved it into the hands of one of the thugs. The man made a show of counting it, then nodded silently. The thugs left without another word, leaving Paa Nii and Shaka breathless and trembling outside the ghetto.

Chapter Four

For three weeks, the boys were crammed into the ghetto with migrants from the various groups. Conditions were deplorable to say the least.

They slept crammed together on a filthy floor, and hardly ate because they were afraid to openly spend their money. They rarely took baths in case someone stole their stuff from their backpacks.

Finally, the day of their departure arrived. Paa Nii awoke tired and restless. He had barely slept at all the night before, thanks to a combination of nerves, and the noise and heat of the overcrowded ghetto.

'Hide the rest of the money in your underwear again,' Shaka whispered to him as they climbed from the floor and prepared to leave.

Paa Nii nodded. 'Okay. Alex said it will take us a week to cross the desert in the pickup trucks. Just keep your water bottle safe and try not to drink loads at a time.'

The group of migrants were now ready to cross the dreaded Sahara. The Sahara Desert is the third largest in the world, but the largest hot desert. The reality of crossing the 9.2 million square kilometre desert was beginning to dawn on Paa Nii. His nerves racked up when he noticed a few people muttering prayers under their breath.

There were about fifteen trucks in the convoy. The ride was hard and bumpy. The sun was scorching but Paa Nii resisted the temptation to drink any of his water. The boys had just a gallon each. They also had some nuts, cereal and fruit; it would have to last them over six days.

*

That night, Paa Nii lay shivering in his tent. He was amazed Shaka had fallen asleep so quickly. The eerie sounds kept him awake; wind whistling across the desert, and the shrieks and rasps of unrecognisable animals. He pulled his blanket up over his head as his mind drifted to the old ghost stories they used to tell at school.

His mind raced all night, and he was finally jolted out of sleep at dawn, by the *passeur* calling out for them to get ready to board the pickups again.

Three hours into their journey, Paa Nii was beginning to feel sick. It wasn't from the scorching sun, but from the horrific things they drove by. Bodies in various states of decay lay strewn across the desert; most of them having perished from thirst and exhaustion.

Shaka was dead quiet; he had been quiet the whole day. It was uncharacteristic for him to be so silent. Paa Nii was worried because his friend was supposed to be the stronger of the two.

The sound of gunshots jolted him out of his thoughts. The truck in front sped off, while some of the migrants jumped out of the pickups in a bid to escape. A couple of Pinzgauer and military Jeeps surrounded the group. It was the military patrol.

The lead pickup stopped, and waved a white handkerchief. Paa Nii looked on in terror as the patrol yanked people out of the leading pickups and began to rough them up. Then, Monsieur Loe climbed calmly out of the truck. He walked up to the ranking officer and gave him a large bundle of money. And then, without speaking, the leader of the military patrol motioned to his men and they climbed back into their Jeeps. They disappeared into the desert.

Paa Nii gave a sigh of relief. He glanced at Shaka, who just shook his head in disbelief.

The *passeur* changed their course; it seemed like he knew the desert like the back of his hand. The journey continued smoothly, though they saw the occasional dead bodies along the way. Paa Nii did his best to block them out.

Shaka's deep silence unnerved him more. They drove for hours before settling down for the evening.

'What's wrong, Shaka boy?' Paa Nii asked. 'You've been quiet the whole day.'

Shaka brushed him off, claiming he was just tired. He went straight to sleep without eating anything.

Paa Nii stayed up a bit. *We're half way through*, he told himself. *Three days to go. God will see us through*. He closed his eyes and slept through the night for the first time since they'd left Ghana.

Chapter Five

The migrants set off in the pickups the next day. Paa Nii was relieved to see Shaka eat something before they got on their way again. It was like he had become a different person since Monsieur Loe's roll call at Agadez.

Maybe Shaka was worried he would run out of money and it had left him disorientated. Paa Nii still had enough money and it was well hidden. He'd told Shaka this several times, but it seemed to have done little to reassure his friend.

The sun was hotter than it had been the previous days. Shaka sipped some water and passed Paa Nii his money, which was wrapped tightly in a plastic bag.

'Why are you giving me your money?'

'I know why.' Shaka always used this phrase when he had a premonition or bad dream. He had constantly boasted in the past that all his predictions and dreams came true.

A few hours into the journey, it became very windy; it looked like a sandstorm was brewing. The *passeur* continued driving, even though visibility was really poor. Paa Nii covered his face with the scarf he had purchased in Agadez. It turned out to be very handy.

Sudden gunshots boomed through the air, drawing the caravan to a stop. Visibility was still awful, so it wasn't clear what was happening. A couple of migrants alighted from the pickups, but were gunned down. Others started running in panic but met the same fate.

Paa Nii stared in horror, his heart racing and a line of sweat running down his back. He glanced sideways at Shaka. His friend was watching in open-mouthed silence. They both stayed motionless in the back of the pickup. Through the billowing sand, they could see that a large convoy of pickups and minibuses had boxed them in.

Men jumped out of the vehicles wielding AK47 assault rifles. *'Allez, tout le monde sort,'* they shouted in French.

'C'est les rebelles,' Paa Nii heard a migrant whisper, as they all obediently scrambled out of the pickups. The *passeur* got down to speak to the leaders of the group. Paa Nii froze when Monsieur Loe was gunned down.

Migrants started fleeing in all directions. The rebels shot sporadically, gunning down a few. They were quickly boxed in again, so no one could escape. Paa Nii was in shock; he had never seen anyone killed before. The sound of high-pitched wailing filled the desert.

Shaka looked ashen. He turned to Paa Nii and shook his head in disbelief.

'I'm Diallo Mende,' the leader of the rebels declared. 'Take out all your valuables or get shot.'

The migrants were told to kneel down with their hands on their heads. All the women were rounded up and put in the rebels' vans. Their evil laughter was self-explanatory. 'Now bring out everything you have,' Diallo blurted. Some gave them all their money and he had men write down their names.

'I'm going to distract them before they get to us,' Shaka whispered.

Paa Nii shook his head. 'Don't do anything stupid,' he hissed. 'I have enough money to pay for us.'

Alex got up and joined the rebels. To Paa Nii's bewilderment, he started speaking to them in French. 'Told you I didn't trust him,' he whispered to Shaka. 'He's an informer.'

The wind started blowing again and the sand blurred visibility. Shaka took off before Paa Nii could stop him. The bullets hit his back and he fell to the ground, dead. In shock, Paa Nii ran in the other direction. A number of migrants followed. He didn't stop when he heard people cry out in pain. Bullets flew past his head.

The sandstorm picked up, but Paa Nii kept running. Though he could barely see a metre in front of him, he ran until the force of the wind knocked him out. Shocked and exhausted, he collapsed into a dune.

*

Paa Nii woke up to two men shaking him and pouring water on his face. He didn't know how long he had been lying there. He realised the men were part of the group that had escaped. They were about six of them left; the others had been either enslaved or killed.

Paa Nii burst into tears when Shaka's demise played on his mind. The men tried consoling him, but it was to no avail. One of them gave him some water and introduced himself as Pierre, a Gabonese also looking for greener pastures in Europe.

'I play dead,' he said in broken English. 'We have to walk the rest of the way to Al Qatrun.'

'It will take us five days or more to get there,' the other man warned. 'Unless we're lucky enough to meet a safe caravan to take us the rest of the way.'

Paa Nii climbed slowly to his feet and looked out across the desert. All he could see were rolling dunes in every direction. 'How do we know which way to go?' he queried.

'I always keep a compass,' Pierre replied. 'When we get to the Libyan border we might have to bribe another group to join them.'

*

Paa Nii collapsed on the hot desert sand. They'd been walking for over three days and were down to their last drop of water. Though Pierre denied it, Paa Nii knew they were lost. The other man had died the day before. He had offered to buy their water from them for five hundred dollars, but neither of them had had any left.

Paa Nii was exhausted. He recited a few psalms under his breath, seeking divine help. He felt like he was about to pass out.

'Look!' Pierre called suddenly, yanking Paa Nii from his daze. He looked up to see Pierre pointing towards the horizon. He could just make out the shape of a few Toyota Hilux pickup trucks on the horizon. Pierre stepped out from behind the dune they were hiding in to make sure it was not a mirage or rebels.

He quickly went through the dead migrant's stuff, looking for the money he had offered them.

'We have to bribe them to join them,' Pierre explained when he saw the disgust on Paa Nii's face.

He found the money in the dead man's underpants. Paa Nii felt sick; it was nauseating for him to see that. Pierre ran up to the approaching Hiluxes and frantically waved his hands for them to stop. He gave the *passeur* of the group four hundred dollars. Paa Nii almost sobbed in relief when they were permitted to join the new group of migrants.

Chapter Six

Paa Nii burst into tears when he finally laid his head down in the room he had rented. After they had joined the new caravan, it had taken them two more days to get to Al Qatrun, the border town where they would make their way to Tripoli.

A few hours after being rescued, Pierre too had died. They had been way off course and he was more dehydrated than Paa Nii had realised. Even though Pierre had bought water from another migrant, he had still died a couple of hours later. Paa Nii wondered whether the whole trip was worth it. After all, it had already cost the life of Shaka.

Exhausted as he was, Paa Nii couldn't sleep the whole night. He heard a lot of people screaming like they were being tortured. It was a sound he would hear every night of the two weeks he spent in the Al Qatrun ghetto.

He spent most of the time indoors. There was another roll call and thankfully his name was called as part of the new group he had joined. He didn't see anyone from his previous group; they were all either dead or enslaved.

After two weeks in Al Qatrun, Paa Nii and the other migrants were smuggled in large tankers to Tripoli under the cover of darkness.

It was a claustrophobic experience. They were crammed up together and there was hardly any air. He was relieved they got to the Tripoli ghetto without running into government ants – smuggling officials.

The Tripoli ghetto was much bigger than all the others he had been to. There were militia – called supervisors – patrolling the ghetto. Some, he learned, had been stuck there for months, and some for years.

Paa Nii had befriended an Eritrean chap in the ghetto, who advised him to look for work among the local populace. It was risky to run out of money at this stage. Paa Nii knew he could be left behind in the ghetto for months or years if he couldn't pay for the trip to Sabratha. Sabratha was the last point of entry before they crossed the Mediterranean. It was 400 miles south of Tripoli.

Paa Nii assured his new friend Isaias he had enough to make it to Sabratha. 'How long have you been in this ghetto for?' he asked.

'Six months. I had to work as a house boy for a very wicked guy, who paid me peanuts.'

In the Tripoli ghetto, Paa Nii enjoyed the first proper meal and shower he'd had for ages. He decided against going sightseeing in case he got lost or kidnapped. His focus was waiting for his new agent to gather everyone in his group to leave for Sabratha.

*

After three long weeks, it was finally time to continue the journey to Sabratha. Paa Nii was shocked to see a large fleet of sleek black Mercedes-Benzes with tinted glass waiting for them. He had been expecting another rickety bus or truck. For the first time, he actually enjoyed the ride in the fully air-conditioned car. Isaias gave Paa Nii a wry smile. Perhaps things were taking a turn for the better.

There was another roll call when they got to Sabratha. Paa Nii's name was on the list, but for some reason, Isaias's was not. He realised the lists had been intentionally manipulated to extort more money from the migrants. Isaias was pulled away with the others whose names were missing. The ones who resisted were lashed with an actual whip.

The cry of pain after each crack of the whip pierced Paa Nii's soul. He looked away, careful to show no emotion so he wasn't picked out as a weakling.

Isaias and the other migrants who had not made the roll call were lead back to one of the Mercedes and driven off. Paa Nii wondered sickly what would happen to them.

He had lost everyone he had befriended during the journey, and Shaka's death in particular had left him half dead. He was mentally exhausted, and he didn't care what happened to him any longer. But somehow, it also strengthened his resolve to cross the Mediterranean. He knew it was what Shaka would have wanted. And at the thought, Paa Nii was suddenly more determined than ever to succeed.

Chapter Seven

Paa Nii had lost count of the days and months. He was shocked to realise it was July; seven months since he and his late friend had left Ghana. The waits at the various ghettos had prolonged the journey. But now it was now time to cross the sea.

Crossing the Mediterranean from Libya to Italy was the most dangerous route to Europe. It was known as the Central Route and had been the cause of thousands of migrants' demise.

The journey usually took three days, and the migrants were packed on the inflatable rafts like a pack of sardines. Most of the time, the overpacked rafts capsized and most of the migrants drowned before they could be rescued by the Italian coastguard.

The news broke across the ghetto that they would be crossing that night. The main agent for Paa Nii's contact in the Libyan coastguard had given them the green light to proceed.

The night was prefect for smuggling migrants. The sky was dark and the sea was still. Three rafts were made ready for the migrants to get onto. Over a hundred migrants piled on to each raft. Paa Nii tried to get a good spot, but still felt suffocated.

A bigger raft with armed men escorted them for a distance and left them after they had cleared Libyan waters.

Paa Nii felt seasick and didn't dare blink in case he fell into the ocean. The life jacket kept him warm and he told himself again and again that this would be over in three days. Most of the migrants slept leaning on each other for support, but Paa Nii stayed awake until dawn, terrified of falling into the water.

There was hardly any wind, but that did little to ease his nerves. He felt thirsty, even though he had drunk loads of water before getting on the raft. He had just a little bit of water left, but took a chance and gulped it all down. Instantly, he regretted it. He would now have to go two more days without water.

The sea was calm, and Paa Nii at last felt a bit confident he could doze off without incident. But after what could only have been a few hours, it started raining, startling Paa Nii from his sleep. The sea became choppy and the rafts began to sway violently.

A big wave lifted the raft so high, leaving the migrants to scream in terror, but the rain stopped as suddenly as it had started. There was an instant calm again as dusk approached. Paa Nii felt neither hunger or thirst; they were definitely in a life or death situation.

By God's grace we will be in Italy by tomorrow, he thought to himself. He managed to doze off again. Once more, he was woken by an approaching storm. The wind had picked up again; it was uncharacteristic for such heavy rainfall at this time of year. It was almost like there was a Jonah on the journey.

The raft behind Paa Nii began to sink, the deafening shrieks and roars shaking him to the core. He could hear children crying out. He turned away, too emotional to watch. This was the first time he had seen children on the journey.

Panic overtook the rafts, the migrants oblivious to their leader's call for calm. A violent wave capsized Paa Nii's raft, and several people were sucked beneath the surface. Others scrambled to hold on to the raft. The ensuing melee caused more people to drown.

The lead raft couldn't do anything to help. The leader didn't want to be caught in the commotion. The only option left for Paa Nii was to let his life jacket keep him afloat.

He was wise enough not to struggle to swim in the choppy waters. The screams of the dying hung in the air. He wished he could block his ears, but was paralysed by the horror he was witnessing.

*

The storm died down just before sunrise. By miracle, Paa Nii was still afloat in his life vest. The sea had pulled him so far away from the other migrants, he was alone in the open ocean.

He said every prayer he knew and just shut his eyes, hoping he would drift to safe waters or be rescued. He assumed the heat escape lessening position he had learnt in a documentary at school.

Dehydrated, he drifted for hours on end; he drifted and drifted till the sun disappeared below the horizon. His heart raced when night fell. He was terrified of the dark like never before.

He wondered whether there were any sharks in the Mediterranean. Unrecognisable noises surrounded him, and he was unsure if they were real, or a product of his terrified mind. He couldn't wait for the sun to come up again.

But the mental trauma continued even after sunrise. He was badly dehydrated and famished. His mind wandered from his mum to Shaka, and whether he would get out of this alive.

He thought about all the banter he had got from his school mates because he supported A.S. Roma. He was teased constantly, and he began to wonder why, out of all clubs, was he so obsessed with the Giallorossi. Maybe it was because of their red team colours, for he was also deeply in love with the idea of playing for Liverpool FC one day. His thoughts swirling, he cried out to the heavens before he fainted with exhaustion.

*

He was woken by the blaring horn of a big offshore vessel. They had spotted him from a distance, and were steadily approaching.

Paa Nii was hauled from the sea and taken to hospital, where he was put on a drip. He was severely dehydrated, and it was a miracle he was still alive.

Even though he was physically drained, his mind remained active, he wondered what would happen to him now he had arrived in Italy. His mind juggled between asylum or deportation. It was all becoming jangled up in his brain. But after all he had endured, the thoughts were far too overwhelming. The future was something he could barely contemplate. Paa Nii's eyes dropped closed as he was pulled into unconsciousness again.

To be continued...

About the Author

Nii Addy Kojo Addy was born in Accra, Ghana. He studied Psychology in University but has since reverted to his childhood passion of sports blogging and writing short stories. *A Dangerous Journey to Stardom* is his first book.

www.ingramcontent.com/pod-product-compliance
Lightning Source LLC
LaVergne TN
LVHW020312110826
845148LV00017BA/2637

* 9 7 8 1 8 3 8 0 7 1 8 7 5 *